JUST ME AND MY MOM

BY
MERCER MAYER

For my new son Benjamin
and his Momma

A Random House PICTUREBACK® Book

Random House 🏠 New York

ISBN 978-0-385-37175-9

randomhouse.com/kids

MANUFACTURED IN THE UNITED STATES

18 17 16 15 14 13

We went to the city,
just me and my mom.
Mom gave me some money
to buy tickets for the train.

TICKETS

I wanted to help Mom get on the train
but the steps were too high.
So Mom helped me instead.

But when the conductor came by,
the tickets were gone.
So Mom paid the conductor
some more money.

The city was very busy.
I held Mom's hand so she
wouldn't be scared.

We went to the Museum
of Natural History.
They had rooms full of
old dinosaur bones.

I picked up a little dinosaur egg
to show to my mom.
But someone ran up and grabbed it.
I wasn't going to hurt it.

I tried on some costumes,
just for Mom.
But the museum guard
didn't like that.

HANDS OFF !

Then we went next door
to the Aquarium.

There were lots of fish
in a big tank of water.

They had some seals doing a show.
Mom got mad because
she couldn't find me.
I ran up front to get
a closer look at the seals.

We went to the art museum,
but it only had a lot of weird pictures
and I was getting tired.

After that, we went to a very
nice restaurant for lunch.
We didn't stay, though.

We decided to have a hot dog from
a stand. That was more fun anyway.

Mom wanted to go to a big store
full of dresses and stuff like that. Yuck.

Mom even made me try on some clothes.
She bought me a new suit.
Some guy measured me and stuck pins all over
my clothes.

We passed by the toys.
I found the stuffed animal
I always wanted
but Mom said, "It's time to go."

We took a taxi to the train station.
I got to ride in the front seat.
The taxi driver drove real fast.
That was cool.

I let Mom buy the tickets this time.
She said she didn't have
enough money to buy more tickets
if these got lost.
"Good idea, Mom!"

We had fun, just me and my mom.
I even stayed awake
all the way home—well, almost.

We slept in our tent all night long—
just me and my dad.

I stayed up with my
dad and let him read
a story to me.

Then we went to bed.

I gave my dad a big hug.
That made him feel better.

We had eggs.

After dinner, I told my dad a ghost story.
Boy, did he get scared!

My dad took a snapshot
of the fish we caught.
Then I cooked dinner
for me and my dad.

We went fishing instead.

I wanted to take my dad
for a ride in our canoe,
but I launched it too hard.

We made a campfire.
I found the wood,
and my dad lit the fire.

We found another
campsite nearby.
My dad was tired,
so I pitched the tent.

I picked the campsite, but someone
was already living there.
So I gave it back.

We went camping,
just me and my dad.
Dad drove the car
because I'm too little.

JUST ME AND MY DAD

BY
MERCER MAYER

A Random House PICTUREBACK® Book

Random House 🏠 **New York**